For Libby Rose
~*J.W.*

For my patient family
~*N.B.*

MAGI PUBLICATIONS
22 Manchester Street, London W1M 5PG

First published in Great Britain 1998

Text © 1998 Judy Waite
Illustrations © 1998 Norma Burgin

Judy Waite and Norma Burgin have asserted their
rights to be identified as the author and illustrator
of this work under the Copyright, Designs and
Patents Act, 1988

Printed in Belgium by Proost NV, Turnhout

ISBN 1 85430 466 6

Mouse,
Look Out!

Judy Waite

illustrated by
Norma Burgin

MAGI PUBLICATIONS
London

The gate no one opened
was rusted up and old.
When the wind blew,
it sometimes creaked and sighed.

And tucked amongst the cracks
of the ivy covered wall,
a little mouse was peeping.

Then silent as the sunset,
a shadow came creeping.

MOUSE, LOOK OUT,
THERE'S A CAT ABOUT!

The door no one knocked on
was battered and scratched.
When the wind came calling,
it sometimes bashed and banged.

And through the broken wood,
all raggedy and jagged,
a little mouse was crawling.

Then down the tangled path,
a shadow came creeping.

MOUSE,
LOOK OUT,
THERE'S A
CAT ABOUT!

The hallway no one stood in
was musty and dark.
When the wind groaned,
long cobwebs stirred and swayed.
And across the tattered carpet
of frayed and faded patterns,
a little mouse was running.

Then softly through the door,
a shadow came creeping.

MOUSE, LOOK OUT,
THERE'S A CAT ABOUT!

The kitchen no one cooked in
was grubby, grey and grimy.
When the wind wailed,
the blinds all crashed and clanked.

And round the piles of pots
and long forgotten cupboards,
a little mouse was sniffing.

Then slowly down the hallway,
a shadow came creeping.

MOUSE, LOOK OUT,
THERE'S A CAT ABOUT!

The staircase no one climbed
stretched upwards in the darkness.
When the wind howled hard,
it echoed with the roar.

And up the giant steps,
with scrabblings and scratchings,
a little mouse was struggling.

Then slinking up behind,
a shadow came creeping.

MOUSE, LOOK OUT,
THERE'S A CAT ABOUT!

The room no one slept in
was jumbled up with junk.
When the wild wind dropped,
the bed seemed safe and warm.

And in amongst the mess,
inside the torn, worn mattress,
a little mouse was snuggling.
Then through the quiet room,
something came leaping . . .

CAT,
LOOK OUT,
THERE'S A
DOG ABOUT!